PRA
MW01015662

Top 10 Romance of 2012, 2015, and 2016.

One of our favorite authors.

Buchman has catapulted his way to the top tier of my favorite authors.

A favorite author of mine. I'll read anything that carries his name, no questions asked. Meet your new favorite author!

M.L. Buchman is guaranteed to get me lost in a good story.

I love Buchman's writing. His vivid descriptions bring everything to life in an unforgettable way.

JUST SHY OF A DREAM

10-11-18

#6

A NIGHT STALKERS CSAR ROMANCE STORY

M. L. BUCHMAN

Buchman Bookworks

SIGN UP FOR M. L. BUCHMAN'S
NEWSLETTER TODAY

and receive:
Release News
Free Short Stories
a Free book

Do it today. Do it now.
http://free-book.mlbuchman.com

Other works by M. L. Buchman:

FIVE YEARS AGO

*T*he events of this story occur immediately after Night Stalkers #3, *Wait Until Dark*.

"*I* can still fly, damn it."

"Dream on, lady." Sara Camron looked down at the pilot's pale white skin. Even for someone with gold-blonde hair sticking out the edges of her helmet, her skin was far too pale—bloodless white. Sara could always talk to patients easily, too bad they were the only ones.

As the CSAR—combat search and rescue—Black Hawk helicopter began cranking its engines to lift from this remote corner of the Polish countryside, Sara scrambled.

The blonde woman lay face down on the stretcher in the helo's cargo bay—with reason. The small, bright worklight, focused only on the patient to avoid blinding the pilots, shone off the woman's bright hair, and her bloodied behind—she'd been shot in the butt. The rest of the cabin was suffused with the dull red light of nighttime operations.

No complaints from the patient about pain though, despite the clenched jaw and sweat streaming off her forehead. Sara wanted to just knock her out, but without any confirmed indication of pain, she had no real excuse.

And this major knew that and was trying to pretend she was fine. Well, you didn't get promoted to wearing oak clusters on your collar points in the 160th Night Stalkers helicopter regiment for being stupid.

There was a deep bullet crease in the woman's helmet. Sara removed it gingerly, but saw no signs of bleeding in the pale hair. The bullet was still lodged deep in the Kevlar. Then she sliced open the arms of the flightsuit to access the woman's arms.

Unit of whole blood, typed and cross-matched in one arm. Unit of saline in the other—once Sara could find a vein—to get fluids up. That would have the added bonus of making her veins show better now that she'd finally gotten in taps and wouldn't need to find them again. The patient was so slender, more like a dancer than a pilot.

And her blood pressure was low with an overfast, but thankfully strong pulse.

"Your commander's an asshole. You know that, right?" Seemed like as good a topic as any to keep the woman conscious. Sara wanted to make sure this patient didn't go dark on her without some warning.

"Only when it serves him."

The response was delayed enough to tell Sara that grim determination was the only thing holding the patient together. One second it looked as if she was out cold, the next she was twisting her head to the side, watching Sara's every motion.

"Who's flying?"

"The pilots."

"Their names," there was still a command-level snap beneath the slurred words.

Sara had to glance forward to remember. She'd been yanked off a flight line in Ramstein and rushed north just in time to join this flight. This aircraft's normal medic was down with a broken leg from an ice skating accident of all stupid-ass things—trying to impress a Danish figure skater on a date was the rumor. Another mud-for-brain from Montana was her own assessment. Out of a whole gender of lame brains, nobody ranked lower than Montana cowboys.

"Vasquez and LaRue," the crew chief answered from his seat at the forward end of the cargo bay. He had a good voice, deep enough to carry over the rotor noise as well as being calm, soothing for the patient.

"Don't know them," the major grimaced, but it didn't appear to be from pain. That's when Sara realized that the patient wasn't watching her. She was lying there, twisting her neck in ways that had to hurt, trying to squint forward enough to watch what the pilots were doing.

"Actually, LaRue is now flying your helo. Donaldson, my fellow crew chief, is sitting as copilot." Again that nice deep voice designed to wrap around a woman on a cold winter night. She had little impression of the chief though they'd been aboard the bird together for hours. A short-trimmed dark beard, broad shoulders, but any other features shrouded in shadow, darkness, and the confines of his helmet.

Sara knew that a Black Hawk required two pilots, but didn't really need them both outside of pitched battle. The crew chiefs were typically flight-licensed for basic test flights after repairs—though they rarely flew beyond the edges of an airfield.

"Oh, that explains it," and the patient stopped squinting so hard at the pilots.

Sara thought about shifting to fully block her line-of-sight to the cockpit, but then decided that was just the kind of asshole move the woman's asshole commander would do and shifted the other way. That seemed to calm the patient down.

Sara'd been flying as a medic for the Night Stalkers Combat Search and Rescue for two years now and eight years of National Guard and regular Army before that. She was used to jerk commanders. As if she'd take better care of their people after she'd been yelled at.

"Your commander sounded pretty upset to me." He'd been merely pissed when he'd landed and fueled up near them five hours before. Sara's CSAR helo had been parked in a Polish farmer's field along with a fuel truck. They'd sat just a kilometer from the Ukrainian border waiting for two Night Stalker birds out on some black ops assignment. Only one had come back across the border on schedule.

He'd landed nearby, with two ominously large bombs underslung—covered in Russian markings. His crew chiefs had made it clear not to approach too close, which had been fine with her and the rest of the waiting CSAR crew. The pilot had stepped out while they were being refueled to glare southeast back toward the border, unmoving for the entire fifteen minutes it had taken. Then he'd stomped back to his seat and flown away, along with his two bombs.

"The other pilot, said he was your commander, called me on my personal phone the moment we reported your injury," Sara wished she'd had an air horn or something to blast into the phone.

"He's so sweet when he worries," the woman mumbled.

Sara wondered whether or not to shush the woman. If she heard about elicit affairs, she was supposed to report them. This woman and her commander? Shit! It happened all the time, but it was way worse than the old "Don't ask, don't tell" rule. It was more the "Court martial their ass" rule.

But it was unlikely that her sole crew chief had heard, or would report it if he did. He was too busy looking irritated as hell. He was scowling at her as if it was her fault they were under a "Don't engage" rule that had his M134 minigun sitting safetied and unloaded. He'd been frowning since the moment she'd boarded—not once lightening up enough to talk to her. Of course, she'd been on her way home after six months in Afghan hell, so she'd slept every second she could. And talking to anyone other than a patient had never been one of her strengths. Talking to strange men wearing a whole lot of pissed-off? Them she couldn't even look at.

Sara continued working on the patient.

2

*S*tephen Brown hadn't enjoy sitting still; it wasn't his forte. Never had been.

They had flown through the Polish winter's night, following two DAP Hawks to park here near the Ukrainian border while the DAPs disappeared over it. DAPs were rare—the most heavily armed helicopters in any military. To see two together would be a good bar topic, if the one-star general in command of the entire Night Stalkers regiment hadn't called in before the flight to say that mentioning this operation anywhere to anyone would earn them lifelong solitary confinement in Leavenworth Military Prison. Sounded extreme, but maybe not. Two DAPs pairing up and disappearing across the Ukrainian border meant something fierce was going down.

The first helo had come back unscathed and continued back across Poland after refueling. By now they'd be all snug and warm on the USS *Germantown* awaiting them on the Baltic Sea three hours to the north. But he and his crew had still sat in the Polish night, fully fueled and no call to order them anywhere.

The Night Stalkers flew a different CSAR mission from any other combat search and rescue flights in the US military. All other CSARs flew with nothing except their personal weapons and a big red cross on the nose. Hostiles seemed to think it had been placed there for target practice —Geneva Convention? What's the Geneva Convention? He'd had enough of playing sitting duck in the regular Army.

Night Stalkers' primary customers—SEAL Team 6, Delta Force, and the 24th STS—operated on both sides of the front line...but mostly on the *wrong* side of it. That meant that where the Night Stalkers flew was far beyond where conventional rescue teams were ever sent, or would dare to go if they were. Night Stalkers CSAR flew in fully-armed battle-ready aircraft—ones that just happened to also have a combat medic and enough equipment on board to set up a decent in-flight surgery. Except when they were under a "Don't Engage" rule like tonight— which made him twitchy with Army flashbacks, just waiting for incoming fire.

Night Stalkers CSAR aircraft typically held back at the edge of battle, because their primary role was extract and patch their people together long enough to reach a hospital. Even the flight into bin Laden's compound had a CSAR craft lurking nearby.

Not this time. This mission was so black that they'd been on a hold line at the border, probably hours back from the action—wherever the hell the action was.

They'd cooled their asses for five hours since the departure of the first helo, including two hours past their get-the-hell-out-of-Dodge deadline. Cooled literally—the stark Polish countryside had no dusting of snow, but the frost lay thick on the grass, their helo, and his flight suit.

On ice until the moment that the second DAP Hawk

helicopter had finally limped over the border and settled roughly onto the field. Ten feet from safe, it had twisted badly, but the pilot had finally thumped it down in one piece—bouncing it hard enough for the shock absorbers to spring it back into the air before finally settling on the frozen field.

The call for a medic had been shouted to them even before the rotors had begun winding down.

Helping Sara unload the pilot had gotten him far too close to the DAP Hawk for his liking. Normally he liked a chance to inspect another aspect of these edgy aircraft each time he got near one. But this time it had let him actually see the markings on the half-disassembled bomb resting close beside the bird. Unlike the Americans, Russians didn't advertise that a bomb was nuclear with garish radioactive signs, but Stephen recognized the type and it gave him the shivers. He decided that, in retrospect, there were definitely some things it was better not to know about a mission.

They had the patient settled on a stretcher in the CSAR's cargo bay, but weren't even in the air when the medic's satellite phone had rung loudly. The commander who'd flown through earlier had called within thirty seconds of the report of the second pilot's injury. Stephen had only been able to hear one side of it, but that was all anyone needed.

"She needs a hospital," Sara had protested. "There are several good ones in Kraków and Warsaw that take US soldiers."

...

"The USS *Germantown,*" which had been their departure point a full three hours flying time away, "is sitting in the Baltic Sea. Sir, she needs—" But clearly Sara was speaking to herself as she'd then hung up the phone.

"He said if any harm comes to her, I'd better start running—fast." She told no one in particular, though Stephen had heard her over their shared intercom.

At least they were in the air now.

Not that it put him one meter closer to solving the problem that was Sara Camron.

3

"*M*ajor Asshole," Sara was still pissed at the wholly undeserved dressing-down.

"No," the woman replied with a worrying slur of tongue. "Major Mark Henderson."

Sara totally fumbled the blood oxygenation test—which involved slipping a sensor shaped like a fat clothespin onto the patient's fingertip.

"You shitting me?"

The woman just smiled to herself, but kept her eyes closed.

No way was that jerk the Number One pilot in all of the 160th SOAR, the commander of the 5th Battalion D Company. "Maybe he just nasties his enemies to death."

"No…" the patient's voice was drifting badly and Sara could barely hear it over the rotors' noise as the helicopter raced north. "He shoots them."

Great!

Not wanting to be his next target, she turned her attention to the patient's ass. With blood and saline pouring into her, her blood pressure and pulse should be recovering, and they weren't.

Female pilots were so rare in the Night Stalkers that she'd only ever met the one who flew the CSAR bird and had now switched to take over the late-arriving helo. Chief Warrant Lola LaRue, who'd been the pilot of this flight, had just recently joined the Night Stalkers.

The only other one…

Sara looked down in shock. That meant the woman on her stretcher was Major Emily Beale, the first-ever female Night Stalkers pilot.

Shit! No pressure. No wonder the woman was a hardass. Not that her ass was bulletproof—which had turned out to be too bad.

Beale lay there with the seat cut out of her pants. Four holes lined up across her two butt cheeks. Truly lined up—the bullet had caught her sideways and passed in-and-out through both cheeks.

"Was this a single shot?"

"*Pow!*" The woman made a shooting motion with her fingers like a handgun—the oxygenation clip foremost like a silencer. Oxygenation was good, but blood pressure said that there just wasn't enough blood in her body. "One shot through and through. My friend Michael, he took care of it though."

"That would be Colonel Michael Gibson," the crew chief told her.

Sara glanced at him, receiving back a nod of confirmation. The Number One soldier of Delta Force had been there to patch up Major Beale's ass. What the hell *had* been going on?

Sara had barely spared a glance at the other bird. It had been painted Night Stalkers black. And had another big scary-looking bomb in its sling. Whatever.

All that mattered was the patient. That was how she managed to survive her days. By focusing strictly on the patients and declining to engage on any other topic, she was usually labeled as dedicated rather than strange and phobically shy.

So focus!

That Emily Beale was conscious or even still alive for that matter, with the amount of blood soaked into the thick towel she'd been sitting on, was a miracle. That she'd piloted her helicopter was unbelievable. The Delta Force colonel had done field patches on her—gluing shut the holes in her skin. Holes that were weeping, but not flowing enough to explain the blood loss.

"How long were you flying after you were shot?" Sara felt an itch that told her if this patient stopped talking, she might never start again—ever.

"Two hours. Three. Don't know. Ask Connie." Barely translatable mumbles.

Nobody flew that kind of time with a shot-up ass. It must have hurt beyond belief. Still, it wasn't enough time to account for the blood-soaked towel.

Sara probed the areas around the wounds, but they didn't leak any more. There were no other signs of blood, just a broad smear down the butt cheeks. She even tipped Beale up to make sure that no blood was pooling from an unidentified injury on her front.

"Uh," the chief perched in his seat was staring right at the major's bare ass.

Another asshole male—the major was wounded for crying out loud.

And her vitals were still dropping.

4

"*D*on't mean to intrude, Camron."

Sara's glare was just as laser-death as it had been in high school. Or perhaps deadpan-death, as if she didn't even see him. But he'd grown since then. Or at least liked to think he had.

"But she started leaking blood when you tipped her."

Sara lay the woman once more on her front, and spread her butt cheeks. Blood flowed out of an open wound that had been covered and partially sealed by the other buttock. She'd been shot twice, once the through-and-through shot. The second time entering only one of the legs, high in the crease where butt cheek met upper thigh. No exit wound.

At that moment, several alarms went off.

Blood pressure crashing. Oxygenation sucked which meant the body was pulling back circulation from the extremities. Her pulse rate jumped thirty beats per minute in a matter of seconds as her heart kicked into panicked overdrive.

And the major's eyes fluttered shut—she was no longer watching the pilots.

"Shit! Put on gloves, Chief. I need you here. Stat!"

He'd never understood what "Stat" actually meant, but he didn't have to be a fan of *Grey's Anatomy* or hear all the alarms going off to know it was time to hurry. He had a moment's hesitation as it finally clicked why he liked the show. Dr. Meredith Grey bore far more than a passing resemblance to Sara Camron. Funny that he hadn't seen that before. Of course he hadn't seen Sara in over a decade—she'd gone to college and he to the Army a year or so before the show first aired. But he owned every season and streamed new episodes as soon as he could get them overseas. Finally, he knew why. The mystical blue eyes and dark blonde hair that—

"Now!"

He peeled off his winter gloves and slid on blue nitrile ones. The first thing Sara had him doing was sliding a piece of gauze between Major Beale's butt cheeks and applying pressure to the newly uncovered wound—about the least romantic or sexy thing he'd ever done in his life. Blood was dribbling everywhere. But when he had the hole covered and applied pressure, Beale grunted in pain.

"Finally," Sara cursed and slapped a morphine shot into the major's exposed flesh.

In moments the major stopped responding at all. Only the beeping readouts indicated she was still with them.

"She shows no sign of blood pooling beneath the skin," Sara sounded as if she was speaking to herself—a habit he'd forgotten about.

"Maybe she doesn't have enough blood for any *to* be pooling."

"It doesn't quite work like that."

But while Sara *sounded* distracted, her hands were

moving like lightning flashes, grabbing supplies from the heavy gear bag she'd dragged aboard.

"Give her another unit of blood," she pulled open an insulating bag and dropped the warm plastic sac into the palm of his free hand.

"Like I have a clue what to do with this." The sac seemed alive in his hand, overheavy, a turgid red so dark it was nearly black.

"Hang it up. No! Don't release your pressure on the wound—I always seem to need a third hand." Even as she spoke, she was doing something with the tubes dangling from the bag and Major Beale's arm. With the blood flowing, Sara rolled out a surgical kit.

"*Y*ou aren't a sicker, are you, Chief?" Sara nearly snarled at him. Just what she'd need, another crew chief who barfed on a patient when there was a little cutting to be done.

"Remember Jeff Lyons?"

"No. Who?"

"Jeff Lyons. *Mr.* Lyons. Teacher. Senior year auto shop?"

Sara extracted a scalpel from her kit and held it frozen in mid-air over the major's buttock. She needed to find the bleeder inside the major or she was going to lose her patient.

But Mr. Lyons…

"I don't have time for this!" She leaned down and tried to see what was going on inside the woman's butt cheek and upper thigh.

She hated this moment. She wasn't a surgeon but, being a combat medic, she might as well be. But every time she had to cut into a patient, adding to their injuries in an effort to save them, it gave her the shivers. It reminded her of the first time she'd ever cut into a man to save him. A vision of spraying blood that—

Focus. Focus.

Not the femoral or profunda femoris or the leg would be cold. Also, if those were severed, the patient would already be dead. She poked at the woman's skin, trying to feel the flexibility of the underlying flesh. Was there a spot where it was engorged with misplaced body fluids that would lead her back to the source?

It was impossible to tell in the helicopter. Vibrations rippled through them all as it raced north—low and fast. They'd been told to stay off radar—which was always a rougher ride—but the pilots knew to smooth it out as much as possible to let her work.

She didn't want to just slash all the way across, creating a bigger wound than the one she was trying to fix.

"Is she out?"

The crew chief knocked on the top of the major's head like it was a front door. "Not an eyeblink." It was almost funny. She supposed it *was* funny, but she'd never learned to laugh—having far too much trouble with just speaking.

"Okay, stick your finger into the hole you're putting pressure on. See if you can feel the bullet."

The crew chief swore hoarsely, but did as he was told. Which earned him a lot of credit. She could see him probing around, then he shook his head.

That told her where to cut, hopefully. Bullets had a nasty habit of ricocheting around inside a body, but she didn't have the time or an x-ray machine to find it. She'd cut in the same spot as—

Jeff Lyons!

The memory crashed in and she slammed it aside—and began to cut.

22

*D*amn but Sara Camron was chill.

Not even a flinch as she sliced into the flesh —then or now. Maybe the old jokes about her being ninety percent cyborg hadn't been so far from the truth.

With his free hand, Stephen dabbed, held, handed off tools, and tried desperately not to watch. All of the old high school memories were coming back far too vividly.

The chain on the engine hoist had broken with an ear-shattering snap, ricocheting off like a bullet. Over six hundred pounds worth of big block Chevy V8 had come crashing down onto the auto shop floor. Pinning the shop teacher by the leg.

Mr. Lyons' scream had shattered the roar of a dozen different machines—lathes, torches, grinders—all drowned out in a moment. Everything in the entire shop silenced by that one sound.

Stephen had been only feet away and had shouted for someone to call 911.

He'd held Mr. Lyons' hands even as he'd instantly

organized a couple of the guys to find another chain and prepare to lift the block.

Then Sara had slid in through the window open against the June heat.

Helena High School's auto shop faced the athletic field. When Sara entered, he looked up to see the entire women's cross country team lined up against the outside, staring in horror as Mr. Lyons kept screaming. Two disappeared below the sill—one to faint and the other to barf.

Not valedictorian Sara Camron. She'd walked up close like some kind of ghoul. The weirdo, silent brain-girl of the school. Always strange, always distant. Staring intently at Mr. Lyons like he was some kind of broken engine.

"Look at the blood," her voice had barely been a whisper.

His terror for Mr. Lyons was building with each inch of the spreading pool and Stephen wanted to smack her aside. Mr. Lyons had been the one who had pulled Stephen out of the morass of teenage bad boys and shown him there were other possibilities. But his shop rules were strict: none of his big brother's drugs, none of his parents' alcohol.

"Clean and sober," he'd insisted. Stephen had watched him throw out too many guys to doubt it.

Hadn't saved Mr. Lyons from a failed chain link.

Before Stephen could tell her anything, she had begun whispering again.

"It's flowing too fast. Hand tools. Where are your hand tools?"

Stephen had nodded at the big roll chest behind him.

"Don't lift the engine yet. Okay?" Her voice was so cool and calm that all he'd been able to do was nod again. Except she wasn't there to see it.

In moments she was back with a wide variety of tools spread out beside her in a neat row and a half dozen clean rags from the shelf. She also had the First Aid kit from the wall—meant for cut fingers, not crushed legs. She gloved her hands, then squatted without even looking at him. Her whole attention was focused on Mr. Lyons.

She gave each tool a quick wipe down with a gasoline-soaked rag.

"Best I've got," she'd spoken to herself. Then to him without looking up. "Okay, you can lift it now. Don't let go of his hands."

As if on cue, the guys had just finished chaining the block again—doubled up this time.

The moment it was clear, the pooling blood had pumped out in a wild spray.

Sara had reached into the fray, set a tie-down strap around Mr. Lyons' upper thigh, and then cranked it tight using the haft of a long-shank half-inch screwdriver. But it didn't completely stop the bleeding.

She cocked her head for a moment.

Puzzled?

"You call 911?"

He nodded.

Not puzzled, she'd been listening for sirens.

He listened too. Not yet.

Sara reached for the next tool and when he saw it, he redoubled his grip on Mr. Lyons' flailing hands.

A slash with a razor knife and the pant leg was split open. Another slash, and the skin beneath had been flayed apart as well.

In agony, Mr. Lyons tried to grab her, but Stephen kept him pinned, hanging on grimly and hoping against hope that she knew what she was doing.

The sound of barfing didn't only come from the

window now. A couple of the guys in the shop were losing it too.

She actually reached up inside his leg with a pair of lineman's pliers, then picked up a paddle-jawed sheet metal clamp. Pulling out a long, slippery tube squirting blood— that he'd later learned was a femoral artery—she clamped the end of it with the wide jaws of the Vise-Grips.

Sara had been gone before the ambulance drivers were done. It had been left to him and a very ill-looking vice principal to calm down the other kids. He'd done the cleanup on his own.

It was the last time he'd seen her other than giving the valedictorian speech on graduation day.

He couldn't get over how little had changed in the last decade...and how much.

The tools were finer, and properly sterilized. Instead of being "safe" in Helena, Montana, they were racing through the Polish night in a thirty-million-dollar combat helicopter.

But here they were, again, both squatting over a cut artery—the first by a Chevy big block and now by a bullet.

"Not there. Put your finger in the hole again," she spoke as if he was a simple extension of her own thoughts and being.

He felt her finger tip coming from the other direction tap his own, then watched it move off as she traced the bullet's path through flesh.

"This way... Russian..."

"How can you tell? You haven't found it yet."

"What? Oh. The damage path. The 5.45 mm has a very distinct double-wave pattern in flesh. The 5.56 creates a single, wider area of destruction. The 5.56 could be Russian or NATO, but almost no one else uses the 5.45 mm rounds."

Maybe there were some things he didn't want to know.

7

"There."

Sara found the artery—not severed this time, just badly cut. She didn't have the training to cut out the damaged section and paste everything back together. That was surgeon's work. Instead, she took a flesh stapler and closed the leak without closing the artery itself.

In minutes, she had the bullet extracted, the little bleeders tied off, and the whole thing packed in antiseptic and gauze.

She forced herself to stillness as she watched the monitors.

Blood pressure, up by five points, then ten. Pulse easing down as the heart slipped back out of panic mode: 150, 125, 100… Still working hard, but it settled below 90. Oxygenation coming up, meant there was blood going to the fingers for the clip to measure.

"I think you can call back Major Asshole and tell him his pilot is going to live."

The crew chief smiled at her as if she'd made a joke or

something. He tugged her phone out of her vest pocket and hit redial.

"Sir. You'll be pleased to know that your wife has been stabilized."

Wife? Major Asshole and Major Holes-in-the-butt were married. And serving together? That was crazy.

…

"No, sir. All the credit goes to Medic Sara Camron."

That was another thing. How did the crew chief know her name? He'd said something about high school auto shop. He must have been there, not that she remembered him. She was never very good at remembering people.

…

"No, sir. I won't put her on the line because she'd ream you a new hole in *your* ass for how you spoke to her earlier. And your wife already has five of them, not counting the incision that saved her life."

Sara would too. Except then she'd be duty bound to fix it afterward.

…

"No, sir. If it was up to me, I'd let her and you'd deserve it, sir. Pardon my pointing that out. Nor will I point out that I'd be glad to hold you down while she did it. Goodbye, sir." And he hung up on the most decorated major in the entire 160th regiment.

Sara could only gawk at him. She wasn't used to men coming to her defense. Ever.

The crew chief reached out and tucked the phone once more into her vest pocket.

Then he smiled at her.

"How…?" No, she knew the answer to that question now. "You know me?"

"How could I not know the woman who changed my life even more than Mr. Lyons?" And he peeled off his bloody gloves—properly, she noted—and stuffed them in the hazardous waste sack.

For the first time she looked at his ungloved hands. She'd know those hands anywhere. They used to belong to a skinny boy in auto shop. A boy who had now filled out with soldier muscle to match those hands.

She looked up into his dark eyes, but didn't recognize those. Of course, she wasn't in the habit of looking in men's eyes—then or now. They always thought it meant something when she did. But she knew those hands.

"It was you."

He nodded.

Hands had always been an obsession for her. At least ever since that day squatting in the Helena High auto shop.

The surgeon's fine fingers.

The infantry grunt's fingers gnarled with hard use.

Asked to identify a lineup of the men she'd mediced, she wouldn't know a one by their faces. But she might well know every single one by their hands.

This man's hands were big, powerful. She'd seen how they held the shop teacher's hands as he writhed in pain. They'd been more than just powerful, they'd been kind. He'd offered little finger taps and squeezes to distract Mr. Lyons from his agony.

And she could picture them now in the blue nitrile gloves, as they'd helped her so assuredly.

Sara forced herself to relax, to lean back against the inside of the closed cargo bay door. The crew chief leaned back against the side of his seat, without rising from the cargo deck. A quick glance, to check that she could see all of her patient's health status readouts—now stabilizing closer to normal as fluids continued to flow into her.

Then she flicked off the bright light that had been

aimed at the patient, returning the cargo bay to the soft red light for night operations. She didn't have to look so closely at anything under those lights—something she'd always liked about the Night Stalkers operating at night.

"What's your name?"

8

*S*tephen practically choked.

"Well, shit. That puts me in my place, doesn't it?"

Sara Camron didn't even know who the hell he was—that seriously sucked.

"Stephen Brown," he nearly spit it out.

She'd left the day after graduation, headed for college and Army ROTC. Four-oh'd in, of course. Probably a full-boat scholarship.

He hadn't had any interest in college. Hadn't even thought of applying.

"*You're* the reason I went Army," he didn't know why he'd bothered telling her. Ms. Chill and Remote could care less.

"Why?"

"You kidding me?"

She shook her head without looking up at him. That one assessing flash of her bright blue eyes had pinned him to the cargo deck—not trusting his knees to even get him back into his seat. Those eyes had nothing to do with chill or remote. Not ice blue as he'd thought, but— Dumb thought.

"Let's see. State champion cross country runner, valedictorian, beautiful…oh, and you'd just saved the life of the only teacher who ever gave a shit about me. He pulled me out of hell and you saved his life. When you said in your speech that you were going Army medic, how the hell else was I supposed to pay you back?"

"You didn't have to do that."

"Yes, I did." And it had changed his life for the better far more than even Mr. Lyons.

"I saved his life. I knew that much," again whispering to herself in a way he wouldn't have heard without the intercom connecting them. "Was he okay otherwise?"

"How disconnected are you?"

"From Helena? Completely."

He'd never known anything about her home life. Or her, really. Except she was the over-achiever he'd finally aspired to become himself.

"Yes. Lyons came back to teach the next year with a fake leg. Still there. I go stay with him on almost every leave." And if not for Mr. Lyons, he probably wouldn't be connected to Helena ever again himself.

"I didn't know." She wouldn't look at him, staring down at the deck.

"Sara? What the hell was—" But he bit it off. Her life had looked so good from the outside… Guess not so much from the inside. Come to think of it, he'd never seen her with anyone except the cross country team—and them only when she was running. She'd walked alone in the halls and he didn't think she'd been in any of the other clubs.

She made a show of checking on the major. Still out. The steady beeping of the machines sounded normal—

after his years as a CSAR crew chief, he knew the bad sounds and there weren't any now.

He debated between waiting her out and telling her to go to hell. The shape of his entire life had been changed for the better by two people. Mr. Lyons had unearthed his mechanical skills and honed them. But without Sara, he'd probably have ended up in a chop shop, parting out stolen cars (and doing time whenever they caught up with him) rather than maintaining helicopters for the 160th SOAR. And she didn't even—

"I remember your hands. Their steadiness. Their..." she hesitated a long time before choosing the next word, "...compassion."

He looked down at his hands. They were just hands.

"You remember my hands, but not me." Weird.

She shrugged uneasily.

"You do that with everybody?"

She nodded.

Stephen opened his mouth, then closed it. His hands? He inspected them again, but ended up no wiser. Didn't that beat all.

The more he thought about it though, the more sense it made. She'd come aboard the CSAR helo with her medic's pack so fast that it was as if she could teleport between eyeblinks—there and then gone. But he hadn't needed to see her name on her flight jacket to know her. She still moved with all the precision and strength of that long ago athlete.

Yet not once had she looked anyone in the eye. Not him. Not Donaldson. The only time she'd really spoken during either the flight or the long wait, outside of giving him instructions, had been to the injured major. Even that had felt purposeful, testing for consciousness rather than conversation.

Meek?

No.

Shy?

If she was *that* shy, how had she ever survived in the military?

By being so competent that—

"How did you know how to save Mr. Lyons?"

9

"*I* didn't. But I knew if I didn't try, he'd die. I just used what I learned from dissection in biology class." Never in her life had she been so terrified.

"Bio class? With Ms. Klein?"

"Yes."

"You performed what the doctor called 'advanced field surgical techniques' with a bunch of shop tools—because of bio?"

"I," Sara didn't know how to explain herself…to herself least of all. "I read a lot. Human anatomy—a couple of books."

"What else do you do?"

She waved a hand at the prone major. Finally satisfied with the readings, Sara covered her with a double layer of blankets and hung one more bag of saline. After a moment's debate, she didn't reinforce the sedative.

"That's it?"

Stephen. Stephen Brown. She emphasized the name a few more times to make sure she remembered it.

Sara closed her eyes. This was the moment where she

never knew what to say next. Raised by her grandmother, who had been bedridden since Sara was twelve, had left her with few tools for communicating with others. Silence hadn't merely become her natural state, it had become her friend. By running at the head of the pack, no one else with her, no one else to even see, she had felt free and alone. Studying hard had given her an excuse to focus on something other than people. Her grandmother had lost speech by the time Sara was fourteen, by which time they didn't need words to communicate anyway. After Gran had died the year Sara turned seventeen, she had been the only attendee at the graveyard. She had lived out her last year of high school alone in the vast silence that had fit so comfortably in the small house.

The Army had been straightforward as well. Medics were always outsiders—no soldier wanted to be reminded that the chance of injury was so high that they needed a trained medic hovering nearby. Easy to be left alone. On base she ran, read, and worked. Each time she was awarded a Good Conduct Medal or promoted for being a model soldier had mystified her.

But Sergeant Stephen Brown's silence forced her to speak.

"I'm glad Mr. Lyons is okay." The words slowly grew easier. "He's the reason I went Army medic. I rewrote my speech because of him. Changed everything."

Which wasn't true. She took a deep breath and forced herself to look at Stephen. The softness of the red night light didn't make it any easier.

"Truthfully, I changed it all because of you. I saw how you cared about him," the words rushed out of her now. "I saw how important it was to you to save him. I wanted to do that for you, then for others. I wanted to save them. I have no one. Never really did. But the chance to send them home to people who cared? Who knew *how* to care? I wanted—"

Why were words so hard? It had taken her moments to understand the changes that saving Mr. Lyons had wrought in her. Yet every waking moment between then and graduation had only captured a shade of that meaning in her speech. It was the first speech she'd ever given outside of a class, and the last. Only by focusing on the importance of that message, had she been able to read it at all, without once looking up.

She leaned forward as the major woke slightly. Not conscious, but an increase of movement. Enough to throw a strap across her back and knees to keep her in place.

It was why she'd never reported a single elicit affair. It was why she'd been so angry at Major Beale's raging commander.

Nothing, *nothing!* was more important to her than getting a soldier home alive to someone who loved them. To have that questioned, doubted, was the worst pain. It would be a betrayal of everything she believed in.

"What about you?"

She shook her head. It was a question she managed to drive down deep every time it came up.

"Sara. What about you?"

Oh…the question wasn't coming from inside as it so often did.

It was coming from Stephen.

"What about me?" But that was evasion. "I try not to dream for me."

Stephen was silent for a long time.

Sara was so sick of being alone. If only she could think of what to do about it. No one understood her silences. Men never gave her time to organize her thoughts well enough to speak them aloud. Yet Stephen seemed to understand.

Maybe… She was jolted by the thought. It might be the first time in her life she'd even found a maybe.

Major Beale awoke slowly and turned to look at her.

"How close?" Beale managed a hoarse whisper, but her gaze was clear. Clearer than any time since she'd come under Sara's care. Awake enough to know that death had brushed by her so very closely.

"You're alive. You'll fly again. Your husband is waiting."

"Thank you. And I'd be lost without flying. But that last part is the best feeling there is."

The best news of all was that her husband was waiting.

Then the woman's eyes drifted past Sara's shoulder and she smiled.

Sara turned to see Stephen reaching out. He took her hand in his.

"I remember your hands too. Such sure, competent hands." His voice was low, but soothing and calm as it had been for Mr. Lyons. More so. She felt no desire to pull back. To hide.

Stephen's beautiful hands had always been her ideal. And now he held hers gently, rubbing a thumb softly over her knuckles.

Beale was right.

It was the best feeling ever.

DANIEL'S CHRISTMAS
(EXCERPT)

IF YOU LIKED THIS, YOU'LL LOVE THE
NIGHT STALKERS WHITE HOUSE NOVELS!

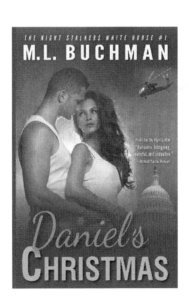

DANIEL'S CHRISTMAS

(EXCERPT)

*T*he phone hammered him awake. Daniel came to in his office chair with the phone already to his ear.

Someone was speaking rapidly. He caught perhaps one word in three. "CIA. Immediate briefing. North Korea."

He must have made some intelligible reply as moments later he was listening to a dial tone.

Daniel rubbed at his eyes, but the vista didn't change. Large cherry wood desk. Mounds of work in neatly stacked folders that he'd sat down to tackle after the long flight. His briefcase still unopened on the floor beside him. Definitely the White House Chief of Staff's office. His office. Nightmare or reality? Both. Definitely.

Phone. He'd been on the phone.

The words came back and, now fully awake, Daniel started swearing even as he grabbed the handset and began dialing.

Maybe he could blame all this on Emily Beale. In the three short weeks she'd been at the White House, Daniel had risen from being the First Lady's secretary to the

White House Chief of Staff and it was partly Emily's fault. As if his life had been battered by a tornado. Still felt that way a year later.

Okay, call it mostly her fault.

As he listened to the phone ringing in his ear, it felt better to have someone to blame. He rubbed at his eyes. A year later and he still didn't know whether to curse Major Beale or thank her.

Maybe he could make it all her fault.

"Yagumph."

"Good morning, Mr. President."

"Is it morning?" The deep voice would have been incomprehensibly groggy without the familiarity of long practice.

Daniel checked his watch, barely morning. "Yes, sir!" he offered his most chipper voice.

"Crap! What? All of 12:03?"

"12:10, sir." They'd been on the ground just over an hour.

"Double crap!" The President was slowly gaining in clarity, maybe one in ten linguists would be able to understand him now.

"Seven more minutes of sleep than you guessed, sir."

"Daniel?"

"Yes, Mr. President?"

"Next time Major Beale comes to town, I'm sending you up on one of her training rides."

"Sounds like fun, sir." If he had a death wish. "Crashing in the Lincoln Memorial Reflecting Pool is definitely an experience I can't wait to relive." The Major was also the childhood friend of the President, so he had to walk with a little care, but not much. The two of them were that close.

"Time to get up, sir, the CIA is coming calling. They'll be here in twenty minutes."

"I'll be there in ten." A low groan sounded over the phone. "Make that fifteen." The handset rattled loudly as he missed the cradle. Daniel got the phone clear of his ear before the President's handset dropped on the floor.

Daniel hung up and considered sleeping for the another fifteen minutes. There was a nice sofa along the far wall sitting in a close group with a couple of armchairs, but he'd have to stand up to reach it. All in strong, dusky red leather, his secretary's doing after discovering Daniel had no taste. Janet had also ordered in a beautiful oriental rug and several large framed photographs. Even on the first day she'd known him well enough to chose images of wide-open spaces. He missed his family farm, but the photos helped him when D.C. was squeezing in too hard.

If he didn't stand and resisted the urge to seek more sleep, all that remained was to consider his desk. Its elegant cherry wood surface lost beneath a sea of reports and files.

Fifteen minutes. He could read the briefing paper on Chinese coal, review tomorrow's agenda which, if he were lucky, might stay on schedule for at least the first quarter hour of a planned fourteen-hour day. Or he could just order up a giant burn bag and be done with the whole mess.

He picked up whatever was on top of the nearest stack.

An Advent calendar.

Janet, had to be.

Well, the woman had taste. It was beautiful; encased in a soft, tooled-leather portfolio and tied closed with a narrow red ribbon done up in a neat bow. He pulled a loose end and opened the calendar. Inside were three spreads of stunning hand-painted pictures on deep-set pages. He took a moment to admire the first one.

It was a depiction of Santa and his reindeer. Except Santa might have been a particularly pudgy hamster and the reindeer might have been mice with improbable antlers. One might have had a red nose, or he might have had his eggnog spiked; the artist had left that open to interpretation. A couple of rabbits were helping to load the sleigh. Little numbered doors were set in the side of the sleigh, as well as in a nearby tree, and in the snow at the micedeer's paws. The page was thick enough that a small treat could be hidden behind each little door.

He shook the calendar lightly and heard things rattling. Probably little sweets and tidbits to hit his notorious sweet tooth.

The day Janet retired he'd be in so much trouble. Not only did she manage to keep his life organized, she also managed to make him smile, even when things were coming apart at the seams. Midnight calls from the CIA for immediate meetings didn't bode well, yet here he was dangerously close to enjoying the moment.

He started to open the little door with a tiny golden number "1" on the green ribbon pull tab. The door depicted a candy-cane colored present perched high on the sleigh.

"Don't do that."

He looked up.

A woman stood in the doorway, closely escorted by one of the service Marines. A short wave of russet hair curled partly over her face and trickled down just far enough to emphasize the line of her neck. Her bangs ruffled in a gentle wave covering one eye. The eye in the clear shone a striking hazel against pale skin. She wore a thick, woolen cardigan, a bit darker than her hair, open at the front over an electric blue turtleneck that appeared to say, "Joy to the World." At least based on the letters he could see.

"Don't do what?"

"Don't open it early," she nodded toward the calendar in his hands. "That's cheating."

He double-checked his watch. "It's twelve-eighteen on December first. That's not cheating."

"Not until nighttime, after sunset. That's what Mama always said."

"And your Mama is always right?"

"Damn straight." Though her expression momentarily belied her cheerful insistence.

He glanced at the Marine. "Kenneth. Does she have a purpose here?"

She sauntered into his office as if it were her own living room and an armed Marine was not following two paces behind her. More guts than most, or a complete unawareness of how close she was to being wrestled to the ground by a member of the U.S. Military.

"Remember what they say about the book and the cover?"

"Sure, don't judge." He inspected her wrinkled black corduroys and did his best not to appreciate the nice line they made of her legs.

She dropped into one of the leather chairs in front of his desk and propped a pair of alarmingly green sneakers with red laces on the cherry wood. At least they were clean. All she'd need to complete the image would be to pop a bright pink gum bubble at him. And maybe some of those foam slip-on reindeer antlers. He offered her a smile as she slouched lower in the chair. In turn, she offered him a clear view most of the way to her tonsils with a massive yawn.

She managed to cover it before it was completely done.

"Sorry, I've been up for three days researching this. Director Smith said I should bring it right over." She waved a slim portfolio at him that he hadn't previously noticed.

CIA Director Smith. Well, that explained who she was. Whatever lay in that portfolio was the reason he'd only had forty-five minutes of sleep so far tonight. And he'd spent that slumped in his chair. He did his best to surreptitiously straighten his jacket and tie.

"You've been researching." Maybe a prompt would get her to the point more quickly.

"Yes, Mr. Darlington. I'm Dr. Alice Thompson, with dual masters in Afghani and Mathematics at Columbia. Which makes me a dueling master. PhD in digital imaging at NYU and an analyst for the CIA. Which means something, but I have no idea what. The reason you're awake right now is to meet with me."

"No, the reason I'm awake right now is to meet with both you and the President."

"The President?" She jerked upright in her chair, her feet dropping to the floor. "No one said anything about that to me."

ABOUT THE AUTHOR

M.L. Buchman started the first of, what is now over 50 novels and even more short stories, while flying from South Korea to ride his bicycle across the Australian Outback. All part of a solo around-the-world bicycle trip (a mid-life crisis on wheels) that ultimately launched his writing career.

Booklist has selected his military and firefighter series(es) as 3-time "Top 10 Romance of the Year." NPR and Barnes & Noble have named other titles "Best 5 Romance of the Year." In 2016 he was a finalist for RWA's prestigious RITA award.

He has flown and jumped out of airplanes, can single-hand a fifty-foot sailboat, and has designed and built two houses. In between writing, he also quilts. M. L. is constantly amazed at what you can do with a degree in Geophysics. He also writes: contemporary romance, thrillers, and fantasy.

More info and a free novel for subscribing to his newsletter at: www.mlbuchman.com

Join the conversation:
www.mlbuchman.com

Other works by M. L. Buchman:

SIGN UP FOR M. L. BUCHMAN'S
NEWSLETTER TODAY

and receive:
Release News
Free Short Stories
a Free Book

Do it today. Do it now.
http://free-book.mlbuchman.com